This book is dedicated to Tony, who's
my hero because without him this story
would have had a really rotten ending.

x X x

EGMONT

First published in paperback in Great Britain 2014
by Jelly Pie, an imprint of Egmont UK Limited
The Yellow Building. 1 Nicholas Road
London W11 4AN

Text copyright © 2014 Kjartan Poskitt
Illustrations copyright © 2014 David Tazzyman

The moral rights of the author and illustrator have been asserted

ISBN 978 1 4052 6575 1

1 3 5 7 9 10 8 6 4 2

www.egmont.co.uk
www.agathaparrot.co.uk
www.jellypiecentral.co.uk

A CIP catalogue record for this title is available from the British Library

Printed and bound in Great Britain by the CPI Group

54090/1

MIX
Paper
FSC FSC® C018306

EGMONT LUCKY COIN

Our story began over a century ago, when seventeen-year-old
Egmont Harald Petersen found a coin in the street.

He was on his way to buy a flyswatter, a small hand-operated
printing machine that he then set up in his tiny apartment.

The coin brought him such good luck that today Egmont has
offices in over 30 countries around the world. And that lucky
coin is still kept at the company's head offices in Denmark.

Agatha Parrot
and the Odd Street Ghost

Typed out neatly by
Kjartan Poskitt

Illustrated by David Tazzyman

Jelly Pie

EGMONT

The gang!

One time **Bianca** went busking with her trombone and got £2.17 and a doughnut.

Martha once pulled the tap off the bath and the water shot out of the window.

Agatha (that's me). There are wet things with eyes and legs living in the bottom of my schoolbag. And that's true.

Mad **Ivy** always says hello when she sees herself in mirrors.

Ellie is scared of non-fat milk because she thinks it comes from skeleton cows.

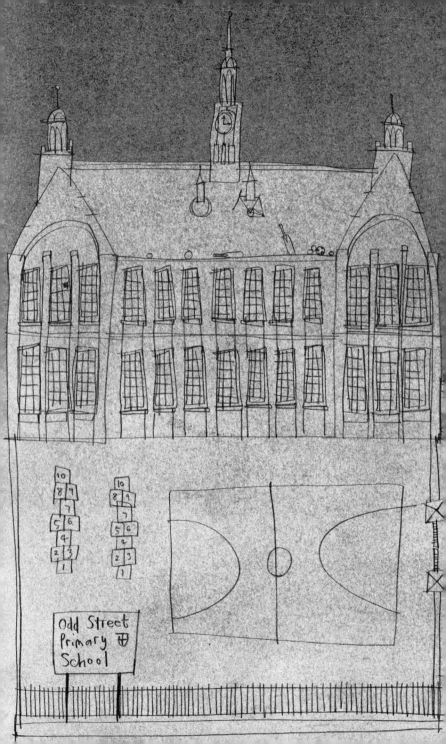

CONTENTS

How to Read
this Book

Hiya!

Have you ever been
woken up by a ghost? I have!

Actually it wasn't the ghost that woke me up, it was the bell in our school clock, but this story does have a ghost so be prepared to be scared WOOO fear fear tremble!

If you want to see where the bell is, look at the pages in the front of this book. You'll see a picture of Odd Street where I live, with my friends and our school, which is called Odd Street School. My name is Agatha Jane Parrot and I live in house number 5, which has a red front door if you want to colour it in.

Our school has an old clock tower on the top and the bell lives inside it along with some smelly pigeons. The bell is supposed to go DANG at one o'clock and DANG DANG at two o'clock and DANG DANG DANG at three o'clock and so on. But one DARK and STORMY night it all went very peculiar, so get ready for some spooky goings-on!

Here are some tips on how to read a ghost book:

1) Make sure you're sitting with your back to the wall. That way, nobody can creep up behind you and make you jump which is what my evil brother James always tries to do. He's just SO predictable.

2) Don't read this book in the dark, because that would be REALLY scary! Er . . . no it wouldn't because if it was dark, you wouldn't be able to read it. Forget this one.

3) Make sure you've got a tennis racket handy, so if a person in a

white sheet comes past going *wooo* (i.e. James again) you can give them a good WHACK! The best thing about this is that if it turns out to be a real ghost, the tennis racket will go right through it and chop it into ghost chips ha ha! Actually I'm not sure if that would work but it has to be worth a try.

Good luck then! Off we go . . .

Midnight Chimes

· ·

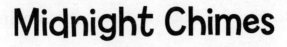

I t was a DARK AND STORMY
NIGHT on Odd Street.

Woo woo woo went the wind.

Whoosh woosh woosh went the rain
on the windows.

Up in the tiny back bedroom of
house number 5, a very charming

and lovely girl* with crazy hair and awesome freckles was trying to get to sleep.

(*That's me if you hadn't guessed.)

Actually I wasn't trying very hard to get to sleep because I LOVE stormy nights, but I could hardly hear any of it because of all the other noises in our house.

To start with, I had my little sister Tilly sleeping on the bottom bunk underneath me going *snore*

snore snore. As well as that, there was Dad sitting downstairs watching the telly *blah-dee blah blah,* the washing machine was going *rum-shloppa rum-shloppa* and Mum was on the phone to her friend Alice going *Yabber yabber yabber oh really? Yabber yabber I told you so yabber yabber HA HA HA serves him right! Yabber yabber.*

I still managed to get to sleep, because the only noise that ever kept me awake was when James used to practise headers with

9

a football against his bedroom wall. BUDDUNK BUDDUNK BUDDUNK CRASH! Luckily Mum told him that if he ever did it again, she'd burn his football boots and make him do piano lessons, so that was the end of that THANK GOODNESS.

So a bit of wind and rain was never going to keep me awake for long. Off I went to sleepy-peeps, but then what DID wake me up was when it all went quiet.

The wind and rain had stopped, Mum and Dad had gone to bed, and Tilly had rolled over and stopped making noises. All of a sudden I was wide awake again staring at the ceiling. Everything was deadly silent and that's when I find it really spooky! You know the feeling, all you can do is lie there listening out for tiny sounds like a skeleton tapping on the window or a snake hissing under the bed. EEEEK!

I was just getting off to sleep again when suddenly . . .

DANG!

It was the bell in the school clock.

DANG!

It was the bell again.

DANG!

That's the trouble with clocks. You can't help . . .

DANG!

. . . counting how many times the . . .

DANG!

12

. . . bell chimes. And another thing . . .

DANG!

. . . our old bell doesn't always chime at the same speed. Just when you think it's finished it does another one . . .

. . . but sometimes it doesn't. So anyway, I had counted six DANGS which meant it was probably six o'–

DANG! DANG!

. . . eight o'clock . . .

DANG!

13

. . . and this book would get very boring if we wrote all the DANGS out, but altogether I counted twenty-seven of them. If every DANG counted for one hour going past then, by my calculations, the clock had DANGED right round until it was three o'clock the next afternoon. That meant it was time to go home from school and I'd missed the spelling test we were going to have. **WAHOO!**

Good old clock. No wonder I went

straight back to sleep with a smile on my face (although I couldn't see the smile of course because I was asleep). (And it was dark.) (And it was my own face and I hadn't got a mirror so I couldn't have seen it anyway.) (This is getting silly ha ha!) (Sausage pie.) (Just thought I'd put that in for no reason!) (I bet the printers take it out.) (The meanies.)

Dad's Smelly Surprise

. . . .

Next morning I was woken by the soft rays of golden sunlight shining in through the window, the gentle twittering of birds, the smell of sausages and a giant plasma telly on the wall showing my favourite cartoons.

That would have been nice wouldn't it? Actually that's a little dream I was having. What really happened was Mum shouting from the kitchen:

'AGATHA COME ON GET UP YOU'RE GOING TO BE LATE YOU SHOULD BE GETTING YOUR SHOES ON AND YOU HAVEN'T EVEN HAD BREAKFAST AND WHAT ABOUT THOSE SPELLINGS YOU WERE

SUPPOSED TO HAVE LEARNT
COME ON AGATHA NOW
AGATHA COME ON!'

Ho-hum. So much for the smell of giant birds and the twittering sausages or whatever it was that I'd been dreaming about.

When I got to the kitchen everybody else was sitting round the table. Tilly and James were already eating toast, and Mum was eating some sort of healthy nutty yoghurt gunk. I plonked myself into a chair and then saw Dad grinning at me.

'What's up with you?' he asked. 'You look awful.'

'The school bell kept ringing last night,' I said. 'Didn't you hear it?'

'No, but never mind,' said Dad. 'This'll get you going!'

He went to the cupboard and pulled out a big box. It was dark blue with a picture of a bright green fish on it. Mum gave it a funny stare.

'What's that?' I asked her.

'I've no idea,' she said. 'I sent

him out to get some breakfast cereals yesterday and this is what he brought back.'

'Looks good doesn't it?' said Dad proudly.

'NO!' we all said. 'But it was on special offer at Spendless,' said Dad.

URGH! That explained it. Spendless is the shop where my friend Martha's mum works and it's full of weird stuff you've never heard of. Mum's always telling Dad not to buy their special offers but he never listens.

'Are you sure it's cereal?' I asked him.

'Of course,' said Dad, passing the box over to me. 'It's called Fishpopz! The new healthy way to start your day.'

I opened it up and sniffed inside. Sure enough, it smelled fishy, but with a bit of wet dog in there too.

'Help yourself,' said Dad getting the bowls out. 'Fish is very good for you.'

'I can smell it from here,' said Mum, wrinkling her nose. 'What else did you get?'

'You DID get something else didn't you, Dad?' we said.

'Er . . .' said Dad sheepishly.

'He's only teasing,' said Mum. 'I saw him coming in with lots of bags. Look in the cupboard, Agatha.'

So I looked. OH NO! There were loads more dark blue boxes.

'Like I said,' explained Dad. 'It was on special offer. Buy one get four free. Come on, let's give it a go!'

Dad poured some Fishpopz into a bowl. They were little grey fishy shapes, and when he poured the milk on, the milk went a bit grey too.

'Would you rather have toast, Agatha?' asked Mum.

'Yes please,' I said. 'But go on Dad, eat your breakfast!'

Dad stared at the grey fish floating round inside his bowl while we had LOVELY toast ha ha! Eventually he stuck a spoon in and took a mouthful.

We were all staring at him chewing away, so he put on a big smile. 'You should try some,' he said. 'Really, it's nice!'

24

He stuck his spoon into the bowl
again, but he was still chewing so he
wasn't ready for the next lot yet.

'Let's see you swallow it Dad,'
said James.

'Mmm . . . mm,' said Dad who
was still chewing, and chewing, and
pulling faces, and chewing. Suddenly
he got up and left the kitchen.

'What's that silly Daddy doing?'
demanded Tilly.

'I'm just getting something,'
said Dad from the hallway with his

mouth still full.

'Liar!' said James, jumping to his feet. 'He's going to spit it out in the bathroom.'

We all charged out and caught Dad sneaking upstairs.

'You don't all need to come along too,' said Dad still chewing.

'Oh yes we do!' we shouted.

HA HA HA!

Sure enough, Dad ended up with his head over the toilet and it served him RIGHT.

'We'll have to chuck the rest away,' said James.

'That's a waste of money,' moaned Mum.

'Maybe we could put it out for the birds?' I suggested.

'We could NOT,' said Mum. 'I don't want them dropping dead all over the yard.'

'So what can we do with it?' asked Tilly.

It was a very good question.

Hmmmm.

The Boy with Cheese and Onion Hair

. . . .

The next important thing happened in school at lunchtime.

At this point, my lovely reader, allow me to introduce my friends and their lunches with marks out of ten for interestingness.

1) Ivy Malting = cheese sandwich and plain crisps (1/10). A boring lunch, but Ivy isn't boring at all, it's just that she can't have anything with bright colours in it. One sniff of a pink iced bun and she goes jumping across the tables. WAHOO GO IVY! We love Ivy.

2) Bianca Bayuss = nutty brown bread thing with olives (9/10). If you think her lunch is weird, that's nothing.

Her mum and dad light candles and read gloomy poetry to each other AND . . . they don't have a telly! No wonder Bianca spends all her evenings playing her trombone like this **BWARB WAB BARP**.

3) Ellie Slippin = some grapes and two biscuits (4/10). Ellie can't eat sandwiches because she feels sorry for the bread being sliced up by a big machine full of horrible knives. In Ellie's magic world, bread would have little legs and eyes and

be allowed to play outside. I have to say, I agree with her. Good one Ellie.

4) Martha Swan = lots and lots of sandwiches (6/10). Martha is big and jolly and she DOES like her sandwiches! They help her to fill the time in between meals.

We have lunch in the school hall but when we arrived there were only three chairs left for the five of us. I had to share with Ivy, Bianca shared with Ellie, and Martha got a chair to herself. Martha can't really share a chair because (how can I put this politely?) if we were all grapes then she'd be a melon.

It turned out that I wasn't the only one who had heard the school bell ringing the night before.

'I counted twenty-seven rings,' I said.

'I counted twenty-eight,' said Ellie.

'Did you count them, Bianca?' I asked.

'No,' said Bianca shaking her head. 'It went on loo tong.'

'*Loo tong?*' we said.

'I know what she means,' said Ellie. 'It went on TOO LONG!'

Ha ha! We love Bianca. Don't always understand her, but do always love her.

'Bianca's right,' said Martha. 'I counted sixteen, but then I got bored.'

'I counted thirty,' said Ivy. 'So I win!'

'No you don't,' we all said. 'It's not a competition.'

'Let's try and stay awake tonight and count the rings,' I said. 'I hope it does it again.'

'Oh no!' said Ellie shaking.

'I hope it doesn't! The bell ringing gave me a bad dream.'

'A bad dream?' I asked. 'Why was it bad?'

'Because it was a ghost ringing the bell, and the ghost was making all the hours and days and years fly past at once and when we woke up we had all turned into little old ladies.'

HA HA HA . . . oh!

We were having a big laugh but then Miss Barking came past and suddenly it wasn't funny any more.

She's the deputy head teacher. She's got glasses like TV screens and she wears hairy clothes and she thinks everything in the world is unsafe. None of us wanted to turn into HER.

Miss B stared at us all squashed on to our three chairs, then she pulled some leaflets out of the big fat folder she always carries.

'That is *not* how we sit on chairs,' she said crossly

and plonked the leaflets down in front of us. The leaflets had HOW TO SIT ON A CHAIR in great big letters, and underneath was an emergency phone number in case you fell off.

'School chairs should have seat belts,' she said. 'I keep asking for them, but does anyone ever listen?'

Honestly! Whoever heard of seat belts on chairs? We all looked at each other, thinking the same thing. We *definitely* didn't want to turn in to Miss Barking.

When she'd gone I quickly changed the subject to something a bit jollier.

'Has anyone heard of Fishpopz?' I said.

'I have,' said Martha. 'They're in Mum's shop. They're so horrible they had to put them on a special emergency offer. What kind of fool would buy a breakfast cereal that tastes of fish?'

I must have pulled a face because they all looked at me then burst

38

out laughing.

'It was your dad, wasn't it!' said Martha. 'So did you try them?'

'I did not!' I said. 'But Dad did, then he had to go and spit them out in the toilet.'

Just then Motley the caretaker came past. He had a black rubbish bag and was putting all the old biscuit wrappers and drink cartons in it. He picked up a bit of squashed sandwich and stared at it.

'Waste of good food,' he muttered

to himself. 'It's still got a bit of ham in there. Honestly, kids today!'

He dropped it in his bag then moved on. But suddenly there was a deafening **BLAPP!**

Over on the far table Rory Bloggs was looking very cross. He'd been eating a packet of crisps when his brother Alfie had come up behind him. Alfie had blown up an empty crisp packet and then banged it right in Rory's ear. Rory had jumped out of his skin and chucked his crisps all over himself HA HA! Actually you shouldn't laugh at boys, it only encourages them.

Rory came stomping over to Motley, dropping crisps everywhere. He chucked his packet in Motley's bag, but he didn't realise he still had a big crisp stuck in his hair! We all got the giggles.

'What are you lot laughing at?' asked Rory.

'Nothing,' we said.

That's when Motley reached over and pulled the crisp out of Rory's hair.

'Is that the new fashion then?' asked Ivy. 'Cheese and onion hair?'

'Yum!' said Martha and we all laughed.

Rory stomped off leaving Motley holding the big crisp. He was about to drop it in his bag when he sniffed

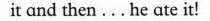

it and then . . . he ate it!

'He ate a crisp from Rory's hair?' gasped Ellie.

'Motley eats *anything*!' said Martha admiringly.

'Oooh!' I said. 'I wonder if that includes Fishpopz?'

The Haunted Cloakroom

. . . .

The next morning we were all outside school waiting for Motley to open the doors. I had a great big bag to give him, full of you-know-what!

We had all managed to stay

44

awake the night before. I had counted thirty-five DANGS. Martha counted thirty-two, Bianca and Ellie both counted thirty-six, and Ivy said she counted twenty million DANGS the big fibber. But whatever the number was, it was TOO MANY DANGS.

'I'm feeling very old,' said Ellie. 'The time is rushing past!'

'Don't worry about it,' said Martha. 'They'll get the clock fixed and then it'll be all right.'

'But what if they can't fix it?' said

45

Ellie. 'What if my dream was right and it IS a ghost ringing the bell?'

Poor Ellie was shaking a bit, so we all gave her a big team hug. Unfortunately we didn't know that Gwendoline Tutt had been standing right behind us and listening. She's the one who lives in the big posh house at the far end of Odd Street and she's really horrible.

'Hey, listen to this everybody!' shouted Gwendoline across the playground. 'Ellie Slippin thinks there's a ghost!'

Everybody ignored her apart from Olivia Livid. Olivia always joins in when Gwendoline is being nasty, so she ran up to Ellie flapping her arms about.

'WOOO!' shouted Olivia. 'WOOO! I'm a ghost!'

Ellie covered her eyes up so she couldn't see.

'Little scared Ellie, knees turned to jelly!' sneered Gwendoline. 'Fancy being scared of ghosts! There's no such thing.'

'What do you know?' demanded Martha.

'Yeah, maybe Ellie's right!' said Ivy. 'Maybe there IS a ghost.'

'A ghost?' said Gwendoline. 'Don't be pathetic.'

'Why not?' said Ivy. 'It's an old school, so it could be the ghost of an old teacher or something.'

'WOOO! I'm a ghost!' went Gwendoline and Olivia together.

Ellie was getting really upset, but

then Motley opened the doors up. Gwendoline and Olivia rushed inside but we all hung back so Ellie could get her head together. It gave me the chance to pass the bag to Motley.

'Here's a present for you,' I said.

'Me?' said Motley. 'What is it?'

'Guess!' I said.

Motley opened the big bag and stuck his nose in. I was standing well back but the fishy wet dog smell was worse than ever!

'If you don't want it, that's fine,' I said. 'I'll just chuck it away.'

I reached out to take it, but Motley wouldn't let go.

'Oh no!' he said. 'I hate to see good food wasted.'

He stuck his head in the bag again and took another sniff.

'Oh no,' he said again. 'You can't chuck this.'

And off he went down to his secret room, which I'll tell you about later.

We went to the cloakroom to hang our coats up. Gwendoline was hanging around outside so we ignored her, but when we came out she said, 'Hey Ellie jelly-knees! You must be right about that ghost. Look, it's thrown your gloves on the floor.'

Ellie looked back. Sure enough, her gloves were lying underneath her coat.

'They were in my pocket!' said Ellie.

'Gwendoline pulled them out,' said Martha crossly.

'I was nowhere near them,' said Gwendoline. 'It must be a ghostly hand crawling about!'

Ellie was shivering a bit.

'She's just being stupid,' said Martha. 'Ignore her.'

Ellie took a deep breath to be brave then went to pick her gloves up. Just as she was tucking them back into her pocket, the sleeve of the coat next to her started moving. It reached up, then a hand came out of the end and grabbed Ellie's arm.

'ARGH!' shrieked Ellie.

Martha stomped over and pulled the coat off the peg. Olivia was hiding behind it.

'WOOO! I'm a ghost!' sneered Olivia.

'That was NOT funny,' said Martha.

'Oh yes it was!' sniggered Gwendoline. 'Honestly, you lot are SO pathetic. Fancy believing in ghosts! We're going to tell everyone.'

Ghost Fever

●●●●●●●●●●●●●●●●●●●●●●●●●

Poor Ellie. She spent the morning trying to forget about ghosts, but at playtime the whole school was talking about them. Even the little tiddlies were running up behind people and shouting, 'WOOO! I'm a ghost!'

Tiddlies are brilliant because they don't understand the meaning of danger. Miss Barking was on playground duty and as usual there was a big mess round the bin, so as usual she said, 'Who made all this mess?'

'It was the ghost!' screamed all the tiddlies, and then they pulled ghostie faces and shouted, 'WOOO!' and then they ran off.

Wicked! If I'd done that Miss Barking would have gone screaming bonkers, but of course she can't go screaming bonkers at the tiddlies in case they all wet themselves. All she could do was look in her folder for a leaflet about ghosts, and then when she couldn't find one she stomped inside for a big sulk ha ha!

Everybody thought it was really funny apart from Ellie, but then I saw something to cheer her up.

Alfie Bloggs had taken Rory round to the main entrance and was daring him to push the button for the

door buzzer and go 'WOOO!' down the intercom. Rory was giggling, but I knew he was scared. I didn't blame him!

If you don't think this sounds very exciting, then you've never met Miss Wizzit. She's our school receptionist, and she is NOT a happy little ray of sunshine. She hates cars parked in the wrong place, she hates wet umbrellas in the corridor, she hates the phone ringing when she's secretly painting her toenails under her desk (I know because I caught her at it once ha ha!), but most of all she DOUBLE HATES people playing with the door buzzer.

'Come on Ellie,' I said. 'Let's get inside and see what happens.'

'We can't just go and spy on Miss Wizzit!' said Ellie.

'Of course we can,' I said. I put my arm round Ellie's shoulders so she could hold me up, then I started limping towards the back door.

'If anybody asks, I've just twisted my knee.'

Ellie helped me hobble into reception where we saw Miss Wizzit standing on a chair. She was trying to fix a calendar to the wall, so obviously Rory hadn't been brave enough to push the buzzer yet.

We sat down, then I did some moans and groans while Ellie pretended to rub my knee better. If there's one thing you can rely on, the more fuss you make, the more

Miss Wizzit ignores you, which is exactly what we wanted. She slipped off her shoe and was using it as a hammer to bang in the drawing pin when the front door buzzer went BZZZzZZzzzZ.

She got down and put the drawing pin on the chair then pushed the button on her desk. She was still holding her shoe with the other hand.

'Wizzit?' said Miss Wizzit.

'WOOO!' said Rory's voice.

'Who?' said Miss Wizzit.

62

'No,' said Rory. 'WOOO.'

'WHO?' demanded Miss Wizzit, giving her shoe an angry shake.

'WOOO! It's the GHOST!'

Miss Wizzit dashed over to the door and pulled it open. Rory and Alfie were running off, so without thinking she hurled her shoe after them then slammed the door shut WAM!

Then she looked down and saw her bare foot with five little toes wiggling at her.

'GRRRR!' said Miss Wizzit.

She yanked the door open again and went hopping across the playground to rescue her shoe.

Ellie was the happiest I'd seen her all day. 'Miss Wizzit throwing her shoe away is the BEST thing I've ever seen in my WHOLE LIFE!' she giggled.

When Miss Wizzit came back in, we were rubbing my knee and pretending not to watch her and trying not to laugh all at the same time, but then it got even better!

Miss Barking came in just as Miss Wizzit was getting back up on her chair.

'I hope you're not going to climb on that chair Miss Wizzit!'

'Why not?' snapped Miss Wizzit.

'The only thing that's safe to climb is a ladder,' said Miss Barking.

'But you've locked the ladder up!' snapped Miss Wizzit.

'I know,' said Miss Barking. She jangled her keys and looked very pleased with herself. 'That way nobody can climb it, so now it's even safer.'

'A chair is safe enough,' said Miss Wizzit.

'Chairs are only safe for sitting on,' said Miss B, then she reached into her fat folder and pulled out one of her HOW TO SIT ON A CHAIR leaflets and waved it in Miss Wizzit's face.

'Allow me to demonstrate,' said Miss Barking and then she sat down, right on Miss Wizzit's drawing pin.

'**YOW**!' she yelped and jumped up again. 'Who left that pin there?' she demanded, rubbing her bottom crossly.

HOW TO SIT ON A CHAIR

Miss Wizzit gave her a long stare then an evil smile came to her face.

'It was the ghost,' said Miss Wizzit. 'WOOO.'

Ellie was laughing so much, it was ME that had to hold HER up when we walked back to the classroom!

The Mysterious Window

. . . .

By the time Ellie and me got to class we were a bit late, but it was OK because our teacher is Miss Pingle who we like a LOT. She's a new teacher and about 100 years younger than the other teachers and she's got groovy hair which changes colour every week. (This week's colour = emerald green. She said it was deep and rich like her personality, but we thought it made her head look like a giant pea ha ha!)

Miss Pingle didn't notice me and Ellie sneaking in because the top bit of the window had come open. It's really high up and the class was getting cold so Miss P was being EXTREMELY NAUGHTY. She had climbed on to a table to

shut it (gasp
shock horror –
how wicked!),
but she was
nowhere near
high enough.

'That's not how to do it,' I said.

'So what am I supposed to do?' asked Miss P.

'You have to guard the door,' I said. 'Then Ivy climbs up.'

'Ivy?' said Miss Pingle.

'Ivy,' we said.

Before Miss Pingle could say anything, Ivy had jumped on to the front desk and then stepped over to get on the tall shelves. She's an expert is Ivy. When we were little tiddlies in Miss Bunn's class, Miss

Bunn was always busy helping the other tiddlies with their paintings, so when she wasn't looking, Ivy used to play at climbing all the way round the room without touching the floor. The only time it went wrong was when she slipped on the edge of the basin. She ended up sitting in the water and had to go and get some dry tights and pants from Miss Wizzit's 'little accident' cupboard! Good times.

In our class there's a water

pipe that runs near the top of the wall which Ivy needed to swing along, and the tricky bit for Ivy was reaching out from the shelves to grab it. If Ivy fell off she'd have landed on the computer, so watching her took nerves of steel. Unfortunately Miss P didn't have nerves of steel.

'Ivy get down!' she said. 'I'll shut the window.'

'But you have to keep watch by the door,' I said.

'Don't be silly,' said Miss P.

'I'm the teacher for goodness' sake!
I'm not keeping watch for Ivy.'

Ivy got down, then Miss Pingle
had another try. She got one of the
small tables and put it on the window
table, then she put a chair on top. We
were so busy watching her climb up
that we didn't notice the classroom
door open.

'Miss Pingle!' shrieked Miss
Barking. 'You're supposed to be a
teacher, NOT a monkey!'

Miss Pingle climbed down and

75

put the chair and table back on the floor. It was really embarrassing for her, so we all pretended to be reading and getting on with stuff.

'If you need to shut that window, you must use the ladder,' said Miss Barking.

'I'll get it then,' said Miss Pingle.

'You can't,' said Miss Barking. 'I've locked it up to stop people using it.'

'But that's silly,' said Miss Pingle.

Miss Barking hissed angrily.

(Me and Ellie weren't surprised she was in such a bad mood. She probably still had a sore bottom from sitting on Miss Wizzit's drawing pin!)

Miss Barking took Miss Pingle out into the corridor and we could hear her giving Miss P a right old telling-off for climbing on the furniture. Of course, as soon as they were gone, Martha went to keep watch on the door, and Ivy was back on the shelves leaping across to grab the pipe.

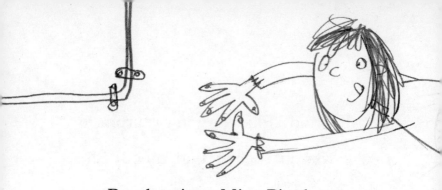

By the time Miss Pingle came back into class we were all back at our seats being good little children.

Miss Barking stuck her head through the door.

'Remember what I said. That window will stay open until . . . EH?'

She looked up and saw the window was shut.

'How did that happen?' she said.

We all looked up and did a big

GASP and pretended it was a big surprise. Ivy even fell off her chair and fainted on to the floor in shock ha ha!

Miss Barking looked around suspiciously, but we were all at our desks, there were no chairs and tables piled up and of course it would have been quite impossible for any of us nice little people to reach that window.

'I don't understand,' said Miss Barking. 'Did anyone see what happened?'

Nobody said anything, so Miss Barking walked round giving us all scary stares. She stopped next to Ellie because she knew Ellie was the easiest person to frighten. Poor Ellie was shivering in fear, but I knew she wouldn't let us down.

'Maybe . . . maybe it was the ghost,' said Ellie.

GOOD ONE ELLIE!

'WOOO! It's the ghost!' said everybody.

'There is NO ghost!' snapped

Miss Barking, but then she looked up at the high window again, and gave her sore bottom a rub. 'Is there?'

Miss Barking went away looking very worried.

Of course Miss Pingle knew exactly what had happened.

'Ivy Malting, come here.'

Ivy walked up to the front. Miss Pingle was pulling her really serious face.

'I want you to tell that ghost never to touch my windows again!

Do you understand?'

'Yes, Miss Pingle,' said Ivy.

'Oh, and Ivy?' said Miss P.

'What?' said Ivy.

'Tell the ghost I said thank you.'

Big cheer and a round of applause for Miss Pingle WAHOO clap clap clap!

She is just SO cool.

The Bell, Biscuits and Bipper Sloots

· ·

That night, the bell went bonkers.

DANG! DANG! DANG! DANG! and DANG! DANG! DANG!

It must have done about a hundred DANGS when I heard Mum

84

get up and go downstairs, so I went to find her. She was in the kitchen wearing her nightie and having a glass of water.

'I wish they'd fix that bell,' she said.

'Ellie says it's a ghost that's ringing it,' I told her.

'Well I wish he'd stop it,' said Mum.

Then we heard some voices outside on the pavement. I looked through the curtains and saw it was

Martha and Ivy with their mums. They had their coats on over their night clothes and were talking about the bell, but then guess who came running down the street to join them? It was Ellie! I never thought she'd be out at night, especially with all those spooky DANGS going on.

'I'm going out too,' I said.

'No you are not,' said Mum.

Then Dad stuck his head in through the kitchen door.

'Come on Agatha!' he said. 'Let's

go out and see what's going on.'

Good old Dad! I dashed to the hall and got my coat on.

Mum gave in and followed me. She took a good look at Dad. He was wearing his old raincoat, and underneath that he had on his tatty bedtime T-shirt and shorts, plus . . . on his feet he'd got Mum's woolly slipper boots which had knitted eyes and little ears sticking out!

'We won't be long,' said Dad.

'Be as long as you like,' said

Mum rudely. 'I'm in no rush to see anyone coming home dressed like that.'

As soon as we stepped outside Ivy ran up and gave me a big hug.

'It's AGATHA!' she shouted.

'Shhh, child of mine!' said Ivy's mum. 'If you shout like that in the night, you'll wake the dead.'

Martha's mum looked at Dad and giggled. 'It looks like one of the dead is already awake!' she said.

'WOOO!' said me and Martha.

The bell was still DANGING so we walked down to the school gates. As we went past number 1, Bianca came out with her mum and dad, which was brilliant because Bianca's dad always seems a bit serious. Not tonight! He had slipper boots on exactly the same as my dad did.

'Snap!' they both said, waving their feet at each other.

'It's embarrassing when your dad wears your mum's slipper boots, isn't it?' I whispered to Bianca.

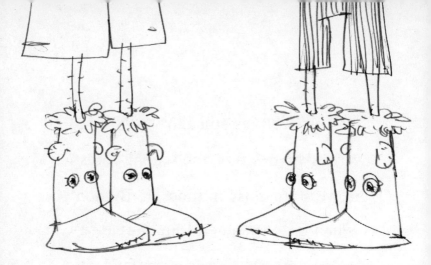

'It's worse for me,' said Bianca.

'Dad isn't wearing Mum's bipper sloots. Those are HIS bipper sloots.'

'*Bipper sloots?*' we all said.

'She means slipper boots!' giggled Ellie.

HA HA HA HA!

I was really glad that Ellie's mum

had let her come out. Being with us was a lot more fun for her than worrying about the bell, especially when Bianca's dad brought out some drinks, and Martha's mum fetched a giant tin of biscuits! It's a bit hard to be scared when you're having a midnight picnic in the street along with two men wearing bipper sloots. We were all having such a good time that it was ages before we realised the bell had stopped.

'It's just resting,' said Martha.

'It does that. It'll ring again soon.'

'Let's all hold our breath until it rings,' said Ivy.

So me and Ivy and Martha and Bianca and Ellie held our breath until the next DANG. And we waited and we waited . . .

'Oh sweet lord!' said Ivy's mum, and she pointed up at the school. 'Will you look at that!'

Something was glowing in the top corner of one of the upstairs windows.

'It's a reflection,' said Bianca's dad. 'The moon or something.'

But there wasn't any moon in the sky that night. Besides, the thing in the window was more of a green colour.

'It looks like a face,' said Martha. 'And it's horrible.'

'There's somebody in there!' gasped Dad. 'We better phone the police.'

'But it's glowing,' said Ivy.

'And it's far too high up for a

normal person,' I said.

As we watched, the face started to drift down and sway from side to side.

Ivy giggled. 'I know what it is!' she said. 'It's a balloon.'

'A balloon with a face?'

'Remember when we made a dummy to look like Martha? We got a yellow balloon and drew a face on it to make the head.'

We all decided Ivy must be right. Somebody must have made a green balloon head and left it floating around the school.

But then the face turned even more horrible and the mouth opened.

'That's not a balloon!' said Martha.

'Then what is it?' said Ivy.

From up in the school we heard a distant groan . . . 'Arghhh!'

'I was right all along!' shrieked Ellie. 'THERE *IS* A GHOST!'

EEEKY FREAK!

Mrs Twelvetrees Has a Brilliant Idea

••••••••••••••••••••••••••••

'**I** shall say this for the VERY last and FINAL time,' said Mrs Twelvetrees. 'There is NO ghost at Odd Street School!'

It was the next day and Mrs

Twelvetrees had got everyone into the hall for a special assembly. Mrs Twelvetrees is our headteacher who is very jolly and sporty and she marches around in big sensible shoes *stomp stomp stomp*. We don't normally get special assemblies, but Mrs T had to do something because everybody had heard about what we had seen, and the whole school was totally spooked out!

Martha put her hand up.

'What was that green face we

saw last night then?' she asked.

'And we're not lying,' said Ivy waving her hand in the air. 'Our mums and dads saw it too.'

'Oooh!' went everybody. They all sounded jealous, especially the boys! It was a bit good actually.

'Humf,' said Mrs Twelvetrees. She looked cross. 'Anybody who thinks they saw this ghost, put your hand up.'

Me and Ellie and Martha and Ivy and Bianca all put our hands up.

'You too, Bianca?' said Mrs Twelvetrees. 'You're normally quite sensible.'

'It was scary,' nodded Bianca earnestly. 'It made my wees go nobbly.'

HA HA HA HA!

'It did what?' gasped Mrs T.

'It made her knees go wobbly,' explained Ivy. 'In fact we all had nobbly wees. I mean wobbly knees.'

Mrs Twelvetrees obviously didn't know what to say, but then

100

Gwendoline Tutt put her hand up.

'I know what the face was,' said Gwendoline.

Everybody turned to look at her. Ooooh, she looked SO pleased with herself.

'It was Mr Motley the caretaker,' she said.

'What would Mr Motley be doing in school so late at night?' asked Mrs Twelvetrees.

'My dad phoned him to tell him to stop the bell ringing,' said

Gwendoline. 'It kept me awake all night, and the night before, and the night before that . . .'

Honestly, what a fuss! She lives at number 59 which is way down Odd Street. I bet she could hardly hear it.

'Thank you Gwendoline,' said Mrs Twelvetrees. 'In that case, would somebody like to fetch Mr Motley so he can tell us himself?'

'I'll go!' I said and whizzed off before I had to hear any more of Gwendoline Tutt's tuttishness.

Motley turned out to be in Mrs Twelvetrees' office. He was fiddling about with the glass tank on the windowsill which is where Tony the school terrapin lives. I told Motley he was wanted in the hall.

'I'm too busy,' said Motley.

'Doing what?'

'Tony's tank's got a leak,' said Motley. 'He's having a holiday in my bucket while I glue it up.'

Sure enough, Motley's red bucket was on the floor and Tony was sitting

in it looking very grumpy.

'I've got just the thing to cheer him up,' said Motley.

He reached into his pocket and pulled out a handful of Fishpopz. He dropped a few into the bucket and shoved the rest in his mouth.

'These fishy chews are very nice, by the way,' he said. 'We love them, don't we Tony?'

'Forget the Fishpopz,' I said. 'Mrs Twelvetrees wants you to come and talk to everybody.'

'Me?' said Motley with his mouth full. 'Talk to everybody? Oh no, I couldn't do that. What would I say?'

'She wants to know if you came into school last night.'

'Oh dear,' said Motley chewing away. 'Oh deary dear!'

Soon me and Motley were back in the hall and he had to go up to the front.

'Aha! There you are, Mr Motley,' said Mrs Twelvetrees. 'Can you

PLEASE tell everybody what you were doing in school last night?'

Poor Motley looked really nervous. He was a bit shy and didn't like being at the front. He just shook his head.

'Come along Mr Motley, we won't bite you! Tell us what you were doing.'

'I can't,' said Motley.

'Yes, you can,' said Mrs T. 'Show some gumption, old chap!'

'No I can't,' said Motley. 'I wasn't

107

in school last night.'

GASP! We all looked at each other.

'He's lying!' snapped Gwendoline. 'Loads of people saw you.'

'How do you know what we saw?' said Martha.

'It was a green face flying around,' said Ivy. 'How could that be him?'

Mrs Twelvetrees raised her hands to make us quiet then she turned to Motley.

'Did Mr Tutt phone you to stop the bell ringing?'

Motley looked uncomfortable.

'Yes, but it stopped by itself,' said Motley. 'So I wasn't in school. Nowhere near school. You can't make me say that I was.'

Gwendoline looked shocked ha ha!

'There has to be a sensible explanation,' said Mrs Twelvetrees. 'Maybe Miss Barking can tell us what's going on?'

Miss Barking went all funny. She opened up her folder and shuffled through all her bits of paper.

'There's nothing here about ghosts,' said Miss Barking. 'And Miss Pingle's window did close by itself.'

'Humf,' said Mrs T again. She came over to where our class was sitting. 'Is that the truth?'

None of us wanted to get Ivy into trouble so we all nodded.

'Well I'd like to see this ghost for myself,' said Mrs Twelvetrees. 'So why don't we make this into a bit of fun? We'll have a GHOST WATCH! Anybody who wants to help has to write a ghost story, and then we'll meet up in here tonight. We'll tell our stories to bring the ghost out. If there IS a ghost we'll see it, and if we don't see a ghost then we'll know that there isn't one. How's that?'

It was 10/10 UTTERLY AWESOME!

The Door in the Ceiling

· ·

After the assembly, it was playtime. I wanted the others to come with me to look in the library because that's where we'd seen the ghost in the window.

Poor Ellie started to shake.

'I'm not going in there!' she said.

'Me neither,' said Martha. 'I'm banned from the library. It's a pity, because those bookcases make great goalposts.'

'That's why you were banned!' laughed Ivy.

So me and Ivy and Bianca set off, but first we stopped by the music room so Bianca could collect her trombone.

'Why do we need that?' asked Ivy.

'If Bianca's practising then

nobody will come in,' I said.

A few minutes later some terrifying sounds were coming out of the library door.

BWARB BWEEB BOOP!

Bianca was blowing her trombone trying to get a new high note she'd never got before. Anybody going past outside would think it was the ghost getting his finger trapped in a drawer ha ha wicked!

While Bianca was busy blasting away, me and Ivy had a look round.

Everything seemed perfectly normal. There were no ghosts or balloons with faces on them or anything like that. We looked up to try and work out which part of the window we'd seen the face in and noticed a square panel in the ceiling.

'It looks like a cupboard door,' said Ivy.

'A cupboard in the ceiling?' I said. 'Don't be daft. I bet that's the way up to the clock tower.'

'Let's find out!' said Ivy.

Next to the window was a big tall bookcase full of fat books that nobody ever read. Before I could stop her, Ivy was climbing up the shelves and the whole thing had started to wobble! I clung on to the bottom of the bookcase to hold it steady, and Ivy nearly kicked me in the eye.

'It's not safe!' I warned her.

'Don't worry, I'm fine,' said Ivy, then she trod on my fingers.

'YOW!' I shouted, so Bianca did

an extra loud BARROOOB to drown me out.

Ivy grabbed the top of the bookcase with both hands, then pulled herself up with her legs flying everywhere.

'Coo-ee Agatha!' said Ivy, waving down at me. 'It's filthy up here. I bet nobody's cleaned it for years.'

Ivy had managed to get herself lying flat out on the top of the bookcase. That would have been enough for most people, but not Ivy. The next thing I knew, she was standing up. The bookcase was wobbling even more, so I had to cling on even tighter.

When Ivy reached up, she could just touch the square panel and push it up a tiny bit.

'Done it!' she said proudly. 'Hey Agatha, if you pass me some of those big books on the bottom shelf, I could climb on them and get in there.'

'No way!' I said. It was bad enough watching her as it was.

'Spoilsport,' said Ivy. Then she tapped on the panel to test it for ghosts, but none came out.

By this time Bianca was going purple.

BWEEP BWURP went the trombone.

'Come on, get down,' I said. 'Bianca can't play much more.'

Ivy started to slide herself off the bookcase but then lost her grip.

'Argh!' she shouted.

I made a big mistake. I looked up and Ivy fell on me along with a load of dust and bent drawing pins and old sweet wrappers and DEAD SPIDERS which all landed on my face. Yuk.

Me and Ivy brushed each other down to try and get clean.

'What's that stuck in your hair, Agatha?' asked Ivy. She pulled out a little grey wrinkled triangle. 'It looks like an ancient crisp.'

I took it off her and gave it a sniff.

'That's not a crisp,' I said. 'I know exactly what it is!'

I'd recognise that fishy wet dog smell anywhere.

Bianca had packed up her trombone, and was standing next to Ivy. They were both staring at me.

'Agatha, you're pulling your hair!' said Ivy.

She was right, I was. It's what I always do when I'm waking my brain up. I needed to know . . .

122

what was a Fishpopz tail doing on top of

the old bookcase?

The Dark Hall

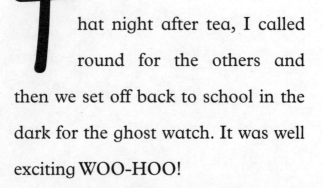

That night after tea, I called round for the others and then we set off back to school in the dark for the ghost watch. It was well exciting WOO-HOO!

The best bit was that we didn't think Ellie would come, but she told

124

us she'd written a really good ghost story and didn't want to waste it. Even though she was scared silly, she wasn't backing out. YO ELLIE – WHAT A STAR! It's always better when the five of us are together.

When we got to the school gates, there were loads of other people already there, but the bad news was that they included Gwendoline and Olivia.

'Oh look, it's Ellie jelly-knees!' sneered Gwendoline. 'I warn you, we've got a ghost story that'll completely freak you out, haven't we Olivia?'

'Hur hur,' sniggered Olivia, which didn't sound nice, but then she never does.

When we got inside there was just Motley, Mrs Twelvetrees and Miss Pingle waiting for us. Motley was holding the main door open, but once we were all in he shut the door and locked it.

'Thank you Mr Motley,' said Mrs

Twelvetrees. 'Are you going to join us in the hall for the ghost watch?'

'Not me,' said Motley. 'I've a few jobs to be getting on with.'

We all dumped our coats in the cloakroom, then went into the hall. It was really dark oo-er! All the main lights were off, there was just a little electric candle flickering away in the middle of the floor and we all had to sit round it in a circle. Me and Ellie and Martha and Ivy and Bianca all huddled up together.

'Keep a good lookout, gang!' said Mrs T. 'Now who's going to tell the first ghost story?'

Ivy's hand shot in the air and she started bouncing around on her bottom.

'Oh me please let me yeah WOW me please me WOW please pleasey-please PLEASE?'

'Golly!' said Mrs Twelvetrees. 'Off you go then Ivy.'

Ivy took a deep breath then put on a very low voice.

'Many years ago there was an evil school receptionist called Miss Wizzit.'

HA HA HA!

Everybody laughed, but Mrs Twelvetrees pulled a face.

'That's not very kind,' she said.

'It's not our Miss Wizzit that we've got now,' explained Ivy. 'This is a completely different Miss Wizzit who went mad if you leant your elbows on her desk when you talked to her, and she kept a mug full of elastic bands to ping at flies and spiders.'

It sounded like our Miss Wizzit!

'Anyway,' said Ivy. 'This evil Miss Wizzit never let anybody use the photocopier.'

It sounded *exactly* like our Miss Wizzit! But before Mrs Twelvetrees could object, Ivy hurried on with her story.

'The evil Miss Wizzit put a dreadful curse on the photocopier so if anybody used it something really bad would happen.'

'Ooooh!' we all said.

'Then one day an evil teacher called Miss Barking . . .'

HA HA HA!

'IVY!' said Mrs Twelvetrees. 'That is not nice.'

'I didn't mean our Miss Barking,' said Ivy. 'I meant another Miss Barking who stopped everybody having fun and wore silly clothes.'

'That will DO Ivy,' said Mrs Twelvetrees. 'Has anybody else got a ghost story?'

'But I haven't told you about when Miss Barking used the photocopier without asking and it printed out lots of skeletons and she was really scared,' said Ivy.

'Oh go on then,' said Mrs T. 'What happened?'

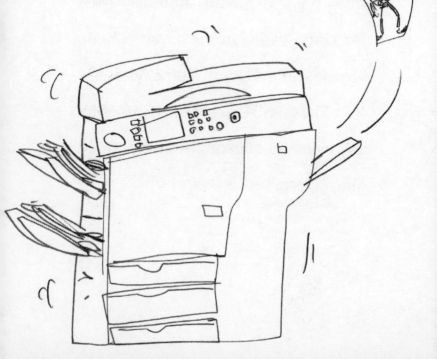

'Miss Barking used the photocopier without asking and it printed out lots of skeletons and she was really scared,' said Ivy. 'And that's it. The end.'

WAHOO! Good one Ivy. We all gave her a round of applause clap clap clap. Even Mrs Twelvetrees laughed.

'You see children?' she said. 'Ghosts are just for making funny stories. Has anybody else got one?'

Nobody really wanted to tell a story after Ivy because she was so funny, but then Miss Pingle noticed Ellie was holding a piece of paper.

'Is that your story Ellie?' asked Miss Pingle.

Everybody looked at Ellie, so she went all shy and tried to fold her paper away.

'Chin up, Ellie old girl!' said Mrs Twelvetrees. 'At least tell us what it's about.'

'It's about a ghost called Nosey

134

Rosie,' said Ellie.

'Crikey!' said Mrs Twelvetrees.

We all cheered which made Ellie feel braver. She took a deep breath and began to read it out.

'Nosey Rosie always used to stick her nose in where it wasn't wanted. Then one time she stuck her nose round the kitchen door and the cook grabbed a knife and chopped Rosie's nose off. Rosie screamed and picked her nose up and put it back on, but she did it so fast she put her nose on upside down. She always hoped that nobody would notice, but there was one thing that always gave her away. Whenever she sneezed her hat blew off.'

HA HA HA HA HA!

We all had a good laugh and Ellie looked very proud. The only person who spoilt it was Gwendoline who pretended to yawn.

'That is the stupidest story I ever heard,' she said. 'It isn't funny. It isn't even scary.'

'That's the whole point,' said Mrs T. 'Ghosts are NOT scary.'

'Oh no?' said Gwendoline. 'I'll tell you a scary story. It's called *The Crawling Hand!*'

Gwendoline looked very smug. I didn't like the sound of this.

'One time a boy was feeling really cold, so he went to hide in the school cloakroom.'

Typical Gwendoline. She was obviously going to make a joke about what Olivia did to Ellie. We could feel

Ellie shivering, but we didn't want Gwendoline to know so we kept quiet.

Gwendoline continued. 'He wrapped himself in all the coats and then sat on the hottest radiator and then . . . he melted away to nothing! The only bit left was his hand.'

'Urgh!' we all said.

'And the hand still crawls round the cloakroom today. If you get too close, it reaches out and GRABS YOU!'

'ARGHHHHHH!' shrieked Ellie.

'ARGHHHHHHHH!'

Suddenly Ellie was clinging on to Bianca. Behind them in the darkness, two people were having a wrestling match.

'Let me go!' shouted one of them. It was Olivia.

'What is going on?' demanded Mrs Twelvetrees.

She lifted up the electric candle. We all saw Olivia lying face down on the floor. Martha was sitting on top of her and wasn't getting off.

'She sneaked up behind us,' said Martha. 'And when Gwendoline finished her story, Olivia grabbed Ellie round the neck to scare her.'

What a rotten trick! No wonder Ellie screamed.

'Did you plan this, Gwendoline?' said Mrs Twelvetrees crossly.

'Nothing to do with me,' said Gwendoline innocently.

'Get this fat lump off me,' gasped Olivia, because Martha had squeezed all the breath out of her.

'What fat lump would that be?' asked Martha. 'I can't see a fat lump.'

'Off you get Martha,' said Mrs Twelvetrees. 'And as for you Olivia, from now on you'll sit next to me.'

Martha got up and Olivia crawled round to sit by Mrs Twelvetrees. She sat there rubbing her ribs and making a real fuss and we didn't care.

'Are we having more ghost stories?' asked Ivy.

'No,' said Mrs Twelvetrees strictly. 'What we are going to do now is keep very quiet and listen. Every time we hear a noise, we're going to work out what it is. Ready? Then shhh . . .'

We all held our breaths and listened.

There was a little bit of creaking from high up above us.

'That's just the roof,' said Mrs

Twelvetrees. 'The wooden timbers are very old and they make a little noise when they heat up or cool down or the wind blows on them.'

Next we heard a car going past, so that was a bit boring. Then we heard a strange bubbling noise followed by a few little squeaks.

'Oh dear,' said Mrs Twelvetrees. 'What can that be?'

We all laughed because we knew it was Martha's tummy rumbling.

'Sorry,' said Martha. 'I didn't

have much for tea tonight.'

'Oh no?' said Olivia pulling a face. 'I bet you had ten pies at least.'

'Shhh!' said Mrs Twelvetrees. 'Let's see what else we can hear.'

'How can we see what we can hear?' asked Ivy.

'Shhhh!' said Mrs Twelvetrees.

It was quiet for a few minutes. But then . . .

Cullink – Clang!

'Eeeek!' squeaked Miss Pingle. 'What was that?'

It was just Motley putting his bucket down somewhere along the corridor!

Slop splosh splupp!

Motley was doing some mopping.

Tooty toot toot!

It was Motley whistling a little tune. We all got the giggles.

'See?' said Mrs Twelvetrees. 'All these noises can be explained.'

Suddenly the lights came on in the corridor and a bright blast shone in through the hall door DAZZLE

145

DAZZLE. It ruined the atmosphere.

'AWWW!' we all moaned.

'Miss Pingle, could you go and ask Mr Motley if he could manage with the lights off?' asked Mrs T.

So Miss Pingle went to speak to Motley and by the time she got back, the lights were all off again.

After that it was quiet for a long time. Mrs Twelvetrees looked at her watch then finally took a deep breath. 'I think we've waited long enough,' she said. 'It's just a nice old building,

and there is no . . .'

ARGHHHHHH!

A horrible scream came echoing down the corridor. We all jumped out of our skins. Mrs Twelvetrees dashed over to the door and clicked all the lights on. Motley staggered into the hall looking as white as a sheet.

'I saw it!' wailed Motley.

'Really?' said Mrs T. 'Where?'

'In the cloakroom,' said Motley. 'I'd just gone in to fill my bucket up, and it was dark so I was feeling around for the tap. And then I got this horrible feeling I was being watched! So I looked round and there it was, staring at me!'

'What was staring at you?' asked Mrs T.

'The ghost,' said Motley. 'It was glowing in the dark. Hideous it was.'

'It must be someone playing a joke,' said Mrs T.

'It'll be Olivia,' said Martha.

'Yeah, she's hideous,' said Ivy.

But Gwendoline and Olivia were

both there. In fact everybody was there. Nobody else had come in or gone out.

'I tell you, there was somebody else in the cloakroom,' said Motley. 'Somebody . . . or some*thing*!'

'We'll jolly well see about THAT,' said Mrs T. She marched over to the sports cupboard and pulled out a chunky old tennis racket, then gave it a few practice swipes SWISH SWOTT!

'Right chaps, follow me!' she said. We all set off down the corridor with

149

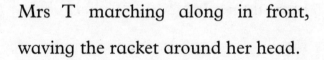

Mrs T marching along in front, waving the racket around her head.

'Come out, come out, whoever you are!' she shouted then she stomped into the cloakroom. One by one she banged open the toilet doors BASH BAM WAM!

In the end it was a bit boring. There weren't any zombies or skeletons or anything.

Motley was waiting out in the corridor with Miss Pingle.

'You've been having too many

late nights Mr Motley,' said Miss Pingle. 'You need a break.'

'There WAS something there,' said Motley. 'All horrible and wrinkled it was. And ugly.'

Motley was looking a bit wobbly. Me and Martha took hold of his arms to steady him.

'We'll help him down to his office,' I said. 'Don't worry Mr Motley, we'll look after you.'

'Good plan,' said Mrs T coming out of the cloakroom. 'And in the

meantime, we'll check the rest of the school. Follow me, gang!'

Off she went waving her tennis racket and everybody followed her shouting, 'Come out come out, wherever you are!'

Poor little ghost! All it wanted to do was drift around pulling a few ghostie faces. It didn't need to be whacked into chips by Mrs Twelvetrees with a tennis racket. I was starting to feel quite sorry for it.

The THING in
Motley's Office

I f you go down to the school cellars, there's a door with a sign on it which says WARNING! KEEP OUT: DANGER. You're getting all excited now, aren't you? I remember the first time I saw it, I

thought it'd be like a mad science laboratory with big blue electric sparks zapping across the roof and chopped off heads in jars with their mouths moving and stuff like that. BRILLIANT!

Don't build your hopes up. The sign is a big lie. It's actually the store room for all the old school junk like football nets, broken musical instruments and costumes from school plays. There's also a table with a kettle and tea stuff on it, and a battered old armchair. The only thing that might be a teeny bit dangerous is the half bottle of milk that has probably been sitting there for 150 years and is turning blue on top. Welcome to Motley's office! This is where he comes for a nice little sleep while we're all stuck upstairs learning 4 x 7 = 28 and all that lot. UNFAIR.

Motley was still shaking a bit when me and Martha got him into his chair. His kettle and his biscuits were on the table, and next to them was a Fishpopz box.

'I'll have some of these fishy chews,' said Motley. 'That'll steady my nerves.'

He shoved his hand in the box but it was empty.

'Oh dear,' he said. 'I must have finished them. Pity, they were nice.'

'Never mind Fishpopz,' I said. 'What you need is a cup of tea.'

'And some biscuits,' said Martha, then she ate one just to test it.

I put a tea bag in Motley's mug, but the kettle wasn't plugged in. There was a row of sockets, but they were all being used. One wire was running off to a lumpy black thing sitting beside Motley's red bucket.

'What's this?' asked Martha.

'It's a heater for Tony,' said Motley. 'It goes in my red bucket.'

'But he's not in here,' said Martha, looking in the bucket.

'I know,' said Motley. 'I had to put him somewhere else. I needed my bucket for mopping.'

Motley reached over to the sockets to unplug Tony's heater and suddenly everything went black . . . and that's when we saw it.

EEEEK!

Actually we didn't shout out, we were so freaked we couldn't breathe or even make a noise. The ghost was there, right in front of us, glowing in the dark!

'Sorry,' said the ghost. 'I must have unplugged the light. Hang on,

I'll get it back.'

The light came back on. There was Motley looking perfectly normal again.

'Motley, is that really you?' I asked.

'Of course it's me,' said Motley.

I turned to Martha. 'It looks like Motley, and it sounds like Motley.'

Martha gave Motley a prod in the ribs.

'It feels like Motley,' said Martha.

'What was that for?' asked Motley

rubbing the bit that Martha prodded, because Martha prods quite hard.

'Answer me one question,' I said. 'Which is your favourite bucket?'

'My red one of course!' said Motley and a big warm smile went across his face. 'We're old friends me and that bucket. We can even do a magic trick together.'

Martha and me looked at each other. 'It IS Motley!' we said. Of course it was. There was only one person in the universe who loved

buckets as much as Motley. (If you want to know about Motley's bucket trick, it's on page 204.)

'Did you know your head glows in the dark?' I asked.

'It does WHAT?' said Motley.

So we showed him.

At the back of the cellar was the props box where they keep all the stuff from the school plays. Last year Miss Bunn's class did *Sleeping Beauty*, so I went and dug out the magic mirror. I held it up in front of Motley then

Martha clicked the light off.

'Oh dear!' said Motley looking at the greeny-white head glowing in the mirror. 'Is that really me?'

'That's you,' I said. 'By day you are kindly Mr Motley, the school caretaker. But when night falls, you are . . . the Odd Street Ghost!'

'But what was that horrible thing I saw upstairs?' said Motley.

'It was your reflection in the cloakroom mirror!' I said.

Motley stared at his green head

165

a bit more, then pulled a few faces and winked at himself. 'Actually, I was wrong,' he said. 'This ghost isn't horrible at all. In fact I'd say it's rather handsome.'

Ha ha ha!

'So why are you glowing?' asked Martha.

'Just a natural talent I suppose,' said Motley.

But then we noticed some glowing dots on the floor. I picked one up, and Martha put the light on to see what it was.

'It's one of those Fishpopz,' I said. 'There must be something in them that makes you glow in the dark.'

'Ha ha!' laughed Martha.

'No wonder Mrs Twelvetrees didn't find anybody else in the cloakroom.'

'I feel like a bit of a fool,' admitted Motley. 'You won't tell anyone will you?'

'Of course not,' I said. 'But what about the ghost we all saw last night?'

'You said it wasn't you,' said Martha.

Motley went very quiet and pulled a little guilty face.

'It *was* you, wasn't it Motley!' I said. 'You were going up to the clock tower to stop the bell ringing.'

'Isn't there a switch to turn it off in the office?' asked Martha.

Motley shook his head. 'It's clockwork,' he said. 'There is a switch, but that's just to wind it up. The only way to stop it ringing is to get up there.'

'But Miss Barking has locked up the ladder!' I said. 'So Motley had to climb up the bookcase. And he dropped a bit of Fishpopz on the top.'

At last, it all made sense. Motley

had gone up to stop the bell and we had seen him climbing down. Then he must have lost his grip and slipped and shouted out, just like Ivy did!

'But why was he in the dark?' said Martha.

'If he put the lights on and somebody saw him through the window, he'd have been in trouble!' I said, then I gave Motley my HARD STARE. 'Well? That's right, isn't it Motley?'

Motley nodded.

'Mr Tutt said I'd lose my job if I didn't stop the bell,' said Motley. 'And Miss Barking said I'd lose my job if I climbed on the furniture.'

'We don't want you to lose your job Motley!' we both said.

'So you promise you won't tell?' said Motley.

'Of course!' We nodded and to seal the deal he gave us both another biscuit.

Martha was just about to swallow her biscuit in one when she paused and put her finger to her lips. She'd heard something outside the door. Very quietly she went over and pulled it open. Gwendoline was there!

'Well, this is very cosy, isn't it?' said Gwendoline. 'Keeping little secrets are we?'

'Have you been listening?' demanded Martha.

'I just want to know why Motley is going to lose his job,' said Gwendoline. 'Is it for pretending to be a ghost? Well he doesn't scare me!'

'He wasn't pretending anything,' I said.

'Oh, so you're telling me there's a REAL ghost, are you?' sneered Gwendoline.

'Yes I am!' I said. 'But it isn't Motley. It's NOSEY ROSIE!'

Gwendoline's big mouth dropped open in shock. 'Nosey Rosie?' she gasped.

'That's right. Ellie was telling the truth, so you better watch out, Gwendoline!'

'You're pathetic Agatha,' said Gwendoline. 'Really, I mean it. SO pathetic.'

Then off she went THANK GOODNESS.

'What did you go and say that for?' asked Martha.

'I couldn't stop myself,' I said. 'Gwendoline really winds me up, and then I remembered I'd seen a mask in the props box.'

'And . . . ?' said Martha.

'I got this silly idea,' I said. 'We

174

chop off the nose and turn it upside down, then we cover the mask in Fishpopz to make it glow. Then one of us puts it on with a hat and waits in the dark for Gwendoline.'

'That is AWESOME!' said Martha. 'Oh go on, let me do it! Please?'

To be honest, I thought it was so silly I wished I hadn't mentioned it, but Martha was already looking through the props box and Motley was collecting the loose Fishpopz off the floor. One minute later, Martha was dressed up and ready so we switched the light off. It was really freaky! All you could see was the green face and the hat. It didn't look like Martha at all. Next to me, Motley was still glowing too, or at least I hoped it was Motley! People look very different when their heads light up. And that's true.

'OK Martha,' I said. 'Do a big sneeze and throw your hat off.'

'Aah-tishoo!' went Martha and

then something hit me in the face.

EEEK!

Even though I knew Martha had tossed the hat at me, it was a lot creepier than I'd thought it would be.

Just as we clicked the light back on, Mrs Twelvetrees shouted down the stairs.

'All clear, chaps!' she said. 'Out you come, it's quite safe.'

Martha took the mask off and slipped it under her jumper.

'You sneak round to the kitchen,'

I said. 'I'll arrange for Gwendoline to come and find you.'

'I'll go first and make sure the lights are off.' Motley grinned. 'Good luck!'

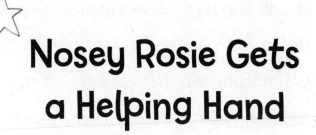

Nosey Rosie Gets a Helping Hand

Everybody was in reception getting ready to go home while Motley went round the rest of the school clicking the lights off. The only person missing was Martha so I told Ellie and Ivy and Bianca what

179

she was up to, because I didn't want them to be freaked out. Of course Gwendoline came over demanding to know what we were whispering about.

'I warned you,' I said. 'Don't forget what happened to Nosey Rosie.'

'You don't scare me,' sneered Gwendoline.

'Please yourself,' I said. 'But you wouldn't catch me walking past the kitchen this time of night. Not in the dark.'

'Why not?' asked Gwendoline.

'That's where Nosey Rosie got her nose cut off,' said Ellie.

'Gwendoline's pretending she's

not scared,' said Ivy.

'That's because I'm NOT!' said Gwendoline.

'Don't believe you,' said Ivy. 'Scared scared scared!'

'Just watch me!' said Gwendoline, and she went off down the dark corridor.

We all held our breath waiting for her to scream. It was going to be SO brilliant, especially after what Gwendoline had done to Ellie! Just for once it would be nice to see the smug smile wiped off her face . . . but then Martha came running up the other way.

'Agatha, we left the hat downstairs!'

Oh potties! I KNEW it had been a silly idea.

Gwendoline came back down the corridor laughing.

'So what was all that about then, Agatha?' she said. 'I thought you were going to have someone up there to shout "WOOO!" or something.

183

Like I said, you're pathetic.'

What a ROTTEN way to end the night. URGHHHH. I was really cross with myself.

'Come along, chaps,' said Mrs T. 'Let's go and leave Mr Motley to lock up.'

'Hang on,' said Gwendoline. 'I've left my coat in the cloakroom.'

'But it's dark,' said Mrs T.

'Do I look scared?' said Gwendoline.

So Gwendoline dashed back to

the cloakroom and then . . .

'ARGHHHH!'

Gwendoline came screaming back out of the darkness.

'It's in there! I SAW it!'

She was completely gibbering and her eyes were like tennis balls!

'Do you mean the ghost?' demanded Mrs Twelvetrees.

'NO!' yelled Gwendoline. 'The crawling HAND! It was trying to climb out of a washbasin . . . and it had horrible little stumpy fingers

glowing in the dark! ARGHHHH!'

She pushed past Mrs Twelvetrees, shot out of the door and disappeared up Odd Street still screaming her head off.

WICKED!

And that's where this chapter ends, so you can shut the book now and save the rest until tomorrow.

Tum tee tum.

Nice and relaxed are you? Jolly good.

Or are you still wondering what

the crawling hand was? If so, don't worry because I'll tell you in the next chapter. I wasn't going to tell ANYONE, but the old man who types these books out for me said you might have nightmares and I don't want that! In fact you can read it now if you want to. It's only a little shortie.

The Little Shortie Chapter

After Gwendoline ran off screaming, we were all left standing by the door feeling completely freaked out. Even Mrs Twelvetrees looked a bit wobbly.

Just then the lights came on in

the corridor and Motley came round the corner carrying his bucket.

'Is everything all right?' asked Motley. 'I heard some shouting in the cloakroom, so I went for a look.'

'Thank you Mr Motley,' said Mrs Twelvetrees. 'Tell us, did you happen to see a crawling hand?'

'No,' said Motley. 'I'm sure I'd have remembered if I had.'

'Just as I thought,' said Mrs Twelvetrees, then she spoke to us all. 'Gwendoline has been playing another of her little jokes. There are NO ghosts, so off you go, gang. See you all tomorrow!'

But we knew Gwendoline hadn't been joking. Her jokes always involved upsetting other people, not herself!

Motley held the door open for us to leave. I wondered if it had been one of HIS hands crawling about, but they both seemed to be fixed on to his arms pretty solidly, so it can't have been that.

But then as I walked past I looked into his red bucket. There was a grumpy little face looking back up at me, chewing on a bit of Fishpopz.

'I see you've got Tony back,' I said.

'Yes, I'd left him in one of the basins so he could have a swim,' said Motley.

Good grief! Tony was about the same size as a hand, and his little legs and his head could have looked like stumpy fingers . . . and he'd been eating Fishpopz!

'So what do you think this hand was all about then?' asked Motley.

'No idea,' I said. 'No idea at all.'

And I didn't tell ANYBODY!

(Well, apart from you of course. Oh, and I had to tell Ellie because I didn't want her to be frightened any more, and I told Martha because I wanted to make up for my stupid

mask idea. And I told Ivy because if she found out I knew and hadn't told her then she'd tickle me to death OW OOOH HA HA NO STOPPIT and I told Bianca because if I hadn't told her then Ivy would have told her, but apart from that I did not tell anybody ESPECIALLY NOT GWENDOLINE.)

The Last DANG!

When I got home, it had got quite late. James and Tilly were already in bed and Mum was having a long bath. Dad asked if we'd seen the ghost again, but I was keeping quiet about Motley so I said no. Then he asked if

195

I wanted a snack.

'Don't tell your mum,' he whispered. 'Look what I got!'

It was a HUGE pink box of cheesy biscuits with a picture of an alien on the front with two heads and long octopus arms sticking out.

'It's Space Munch!' he said.

'From Spendless?' I asked.

Dad nodded. 'Special offer.'

'No way,' I said.

'Oh come on,' said Dad. 'It can't be as bad as that last stuff.'

But sure enough, he tried a bit,
and chewed it and chewed it.

'I give in,' said Dad. 'Maybe Mr
Motley wants it?'

Hmmm. I looked at the picture on

the box and tried to imagine Motley with two heads and octopus arms. Not pretty.

'I don't think we'll risk it!' I said.

So up I went to bed and that was the end of that. I must have gone straight to sleep because before I knew it there was a great big . . .

DANG!

I'd forgotten. A man had come in to fix the school clock that afternoon, and he'd got his own ladder!

DANG!

Everything else was dead quiet, so I guessed it was midnight.

DANG!

I had to laugh because I knew Bianca, Martha, Ivy and Ellie would all be lying awake listening and counting too!

DANG!

The bell was ringing perfectly. It made me feel a bit sad actually.

DANG!

It had been quite nice to think

there was a ghost in the old school.

DANG!

After all, it didn't hurt anybody

and we'd all had a good laugh!

DANG!

That was the seventh DANG,

and it wasn't being very exciting.

DANG!

I knew exactly when the next

DANG would come and it was now...

DANG!

See? Where's the fun in that?

Sorry old clock, you've got boring.

DANG!

That was number ten. YAWN! Just two more to go, then that's the end of the story.

DANG!

Thanks for reading about our ghost. I hope it didn't scare you, but if it did, don't worry! We're just about to finish with one last . . .

DANG!

There, that was it, there is no more. Goodnight, GOODBYEEEE and have sweet dreams because this is

201

THE END.

Motley's Magic Bucket Trick

(Wahoo! We love it.)

How can you have a bucket of water upside down over your head and not get wet?

This is really freaky, because the bucket doesn't have a lid on or anything like that! Motley showed me this with his big red bucket, but if you have a small plastic bucket you can try it yourself.

Put a little bit of water in the bucket then hold it by the handle. Start to swing the bucket backwards and forwards, doing bigger and bigger swings.

Warning: you have to DO THIS OUTSIDE with lots of space around you otherwise you might whack the telly or your mum or your dog or something.

When you're feeling brave, give it a great BIG swing so it goes right round upside down over the top of your head. If you do it fast enough, the water stays inside!

Here's the good bit. One time James was doing this trick, and he wanted me to take a photo! I got the camera ready, then when the bucket was going over his head I told him to hold it a second while I pushed the button. So he stopped the bucket and the water all fell out SPLOOSH. It was the best photo I ever took HA HA wicked!

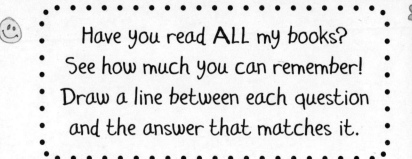

1. Who was told to stick her head in a jelly?

2. Who went up to Gwendoline and did a little poop right in front her?

3. Who lives at 59 Odd Street?

4. Who had cheese and onion hair?

5. Who had a jammy tummy button?

6. Who tried to fly with an umbrella at her fairy party?

7. Who had flying trousers?

8. Who loves her stapler?

9. Who had a green moustache?

10. Who had a matching car and shoes?

11. Who said she had 'nobbly wees'?

12. Who had a scary dream about mushrooms?

Random

Bianca

Auntie Zoe

Bubbles

Miss Barking

Ivy

Rory Bloggs

Ellie

Martha's Uncle Geoff

Gwendoline

Miss Wizzit

Motley

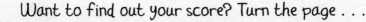

Want to find out your score? Turn the page . . .

Shhh! Here are the answers!

1. Miss Barking, 2. Random, 3. Gwendoline,
4. Rory Bloggs, 5. Bubbles, 6. Ivy,
7. Martha's Uncle Geoff, 8. Miss Wizzit,
9. Motley, 10. Auntie Zoe, 11. Bianca, 12. Ellie

Score:

0-4: Read them again!

5-7: Pretty good.

8-10: That's awesome.

11: Just one wrong? How irritating ha ha!

12: PERFECT BRILL WICKED!

Hiya, Agatha here!

Want to read more about ME?

These are all my books, I hope they make you laugh.

Wooooohooooo!

Agatha Parrot xxx

Agatha Parrot and the Floating Head
Kjartan Poskitt
Tons of Mr Gum will love the *TES Magazine*
Illustrated by David Tazzyman

Agatha Parrot and the Mushroom Boy
Kjartan Poskitt
Illustrated by David Tazzyman

Agatha Parrot and the Zombie Bird
Kjartan Poskitt
Illustrated by David Tazzyman

Agatha Parrot and the Heart of Mud
Kjartan Poskitt
Illustrated by David Tazzyman

Agatha Parrot and the Thirteenth Chicken
Kjartan Poskitt
Illustrated by David Tazzyman

Agatha Parrot and the Odd Street Ghost
Kjartan Poskitt
Illustrated by David Tazzyman

'Full of mischief and wit'
THE TELEGRAPH

'I loved this book and read it in two goes because I could not put it down'
EMMA WEIR, AGE 7

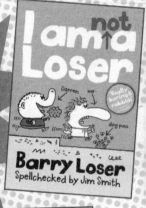

GET YOUR WOBBLE ON AT
JELLY PIE CENTRAL
.CO.UK

WELCOME TO A WORLD OF SILLY JOKES
WACKY GAMES & CRAZY VIDEOS!

Get the FREE app!